Beyond 'Ōhi'a Valley
ADVENTURES IN A HAWAIIAN RAINFOREST

Story by Lisa Matsumoto

Paintings by Michael Furuya

Lehua, Inc.

First published in 1996 by Lehua, Inc. P. O. Box 4, Aiea, Hawaii 96701-0004, USA .

Printed in China

3 5 7 9 10 8 6 4

ISBN: 0-9647491-2-2

Library of Congress Catalog Card Number: 96-94714

Book design: Darryl Furuya

Acknowledgments

Jodi Belknap
Betsy Harrison Gagné
Neal L. Evenhuis
Gordon M. Nishida
Leigh Sturgeon
Lori Nasu
Rainbows & Dreams
Tammy Hunt
Stacey Naki
Tom Cummings
FCI Communications
Alec Shimizu
Angela Angel
Scott Baron

For Howard   Thank you for your constant love and support.
This is for the many adventures we've shared and to those yet to come.
L.M.

Dorinda, Avis and Alice, thanks for the big picture.
M.F.

Long, long ago in Hawai'i there was a beautiful valley filled with tall 'ōhi'a trees stretching far as the eye could see. It was called 'Ōhi'a Valley. In this valley there was one tree that stood high above the rest. For centuries it provided food, shelter and protection to many of the creatures in the forest. It was known to all as the Great 'Ōhi'a Tree.

Hidden deep within its branches was an adventurous young tree snail named Kāhuli. Unlike the other tree snails who were content to remain on the safe strong branches of the Great ʻŌhiʻa Tree, Kāhuli longed for adventure. Everyday he would climb to the top of the tree to gaze at the vast valley below and dream . . .

"Just once, I wish I could go out there and see the world instead of being stuck on this boring old tree."

One day, great clouds covered the sky and the winds swayed the Great ʻŌhiʻa Tree. Kāhuli hurried up the branches, excited by the leaves rustling around him. At the top, he planted himself firmly on a leaf to keep from being blown away.

Suddenly, a strong gust of wind swept his leaf high into the air. The current carried him far above the valley. He was exhilarated by the cool air rushing against his face as he soared over the ridges and valleys, surfing on the wind. He was so busy having fun he didn't even think of how he would land. Then as quickly as the winds had come, they subsided.

"Ahhhhhhh!" he screamed as he fell, tumbling to the ground below until he landed with a . . .

*. . . **thud!*** Luckily, he fell on a soft bed of leaves, the same leaves under which Hauʻoli the happy-face spider had just finished building his web. Hauʻoli rushed over. "Oh no! Look at my house!" he exclaimed.

"I guess your house broke my fall," Kāhuli said apologetically.

"And it looks like your *fall* broke my ***house!***" Hauʻoli grumbled. "I guess I'll just have to build another one." Hauʻoli looked curiously at Kāhuli. "So, what's a nice little tree snail like you doing in Hāpuʻu Valley anyway?" he asked.

"I'm searching for adventure!" Kāhuli replied excitedly.

"Adventure, huh? Well, you'll find more than enough of it here, that's for sure. But this is no place for a tree snail, so it's best you head straight home."

"Home? To that boring old tree? That's the last place I want to go."

"But that's where you belong. Let me tell you something kid, don't mess around with nature. If you were put in a tree, then it's best you stay there. Here in Hāpuʻu Valley we learned that the hard way. Our valley didn't always look like this, you know."

"It didn't?" Kāhuli asked, noticing the destroyed forest around him.

"Oh, no. It was once a beautiful rainforest, with tall green trees and hāpuʻu ferns everywhere. Now this is all that's left because creatures came here when they didn't belong."

"How do you know I don't belong here?"

"Because there are no tree snails left in Hāpuʻu Valley."

"Yeah, right." Kāhuli said rather skeptically.

"You don't believe me? Come see for yourself."

Hauʻoli then led Kāhuli up toward the mountains until they finally reached . . .

. . . **Shadow Ridge**.

Kāhuli strained his eyes to see through the mist and thick fog that rolled in.

"What's here?" Kāhuli asked curiously.

"Not much of anything is left anymore, but it used to be the home of thousands of tree snails." Hau'oli replied sadly.

As the fog slowly cleared Kāhuli began to see the silhouettes of many shells.

"Look Hau'oli, you were wrong! The snails are still here!"

Kāhuli rushed toward them eager to make new friends.

But when he drew nearer he was horrified to find that all that remained of the snails were their discarded shells. The ridge had become a deserted snail graveyard.

Tears filled Kāhuli's eyes.

"What happened to them?"

He was answered by an unfamiliar voice.

Kāhuli turned to see Rosy, a huge menacing snail slithering toward them.

"I thought you said there weren't any snails left in this valley?" Kāhuli asked fearfully as he looked upon Rosy's sinister face.

"I said there weren't any *tree* snails," Hauʻoli explained. "She happens to be a *cannibal* snail. Let's get out of here!"

Kāhuli tried his best to hurry with Hauʻoli pushing him as hard as he could from behind.

"Faster Kāhuli, she's gaining on us!"

"I'm going as fast as I can," Kāhuli panted. "I am a snail, you know!"

"Well, you're going to be escargot, if you don't move faster."

With that thought, Kāhuli pulled himself with all his might. At last, they were leaving Rosy behind.

Just when they thought they were out of danger, they found themselves blocked by an immense hollow log. Kāhuli's heart dropped. There was no way around it and Rosy was closing in on them. They were trapped.

"What do we do now?" Kāhuli asked in desperation.

"Don't worry kid," Hauʻoli said boldly, "She'll have to deal with me!"

Rosy slithered closer as Hauʻoli jumped out and shouted, "I'll have you know that all of these eight legs are registered lethal weapons! Ha-ya!"

Suddenly, fear struck Rosy's eyes. She quickly turned to retreat.

"See," Hauʻoli boasted, looking rather smug, "nobody messes with me!" Just then a large, dark shadow crept from behind . . .

Hauʻoli and Kāhuli slowly turned around. They were terrified as they stared into the glowing eyes of a pack of rats climbing over the log. They quickly hid themselves under the decaying leaves in the hollow, hoping to remain unnoticed. As the rats chased after Rosy, they made their escape down the ridge.

Tired and out of breath, they reached a mountain stream.

"Whew! We're finally safe," Hauʻoli said with a sigh of relief. "The rats will never find us now."

Just then, Kāhuli heard rustling from a nearby bush. "Are you sure?" he questioned.

"Positive!" Hauʻoli replied confidently.

All of a sudden, the pack of rats leaped out from the bushes.

"Then again, I could be wrong," Hauʻoli exclaimed as he searched for a place to hide. Having nowhere else to turn, they sought refuge on a fallen tree which jutted over the rushing stream.

The largest of the rats stalked them as they inched their way down the withered branch. They trembled as the rat's gaping jaws drew nearer. There was nowhere left to go, another step would send them plummeting into the water below. They tightly closed their eyes as they felt the rat's hot breath upon them.

Crack!

The weight of the rat broke the branch causing them to fall into the rushing water. Kāhuli and Hauʻoli clung desperately to the branch as it drifted downstream. Meanwhile the rat, unable to fight the rushing current, sank to its watery grave.

"Now *that* was close," Hauʻoli said as they floated downstream. "Well, that's life in Hāpuʻu Valley."

"It's nothing like that back home," Kāhuli remarked. "We don't have anything like rats or cannibal snails."

"And you better hope they never get there. They've caused a lot of damage to our valley."

"Because they didn't belong, right?" Kāhuli added, slowly beginning to understand.

"That's right, Kāhuli. And that's why we have to get you home."

"That's fine with me, I've had enough excitement for today."

"Well, our troubles are behind us, from here it'll be smooth sailing," Hauʻoli reassured him as he laid back for a nap.

Just then they heard a rumbling sound in the distance. "What's that?" Kāhuli asked.

"Don't worry, it's probably nothing," Hauʻoli replied.

The sound seemed to be getting closer. Kāhuli began to feel uneasy as their branch picked up speed. Before they knew it, the stream turned into . . .

...a waterfall!

The branch flew off the cliff's edge, hurling them into the air. They screamed as they fell through the mist, finally plunging into the tumbling water. They held their breath and struggled to reach the surface, but the current was too strong. Soon their air would run out. They feared the worst.

Before they realized it, something swam under them. It was an 'o'opu who lived in the mountain stream. "Hold on," the 'o'opu called out as he leaped to the surface with Kāhuli and Hau'oli on his back, gasping for air.

"We can't thank you enough," Hau'oli said gratefully as they were brought to safety.

"It was my pleasure," the 'o'opu replied with a smile. Then with a friendly wave of his tail, he quickly dove back into the cool water.

On land, Hau'oli looked for a nice spot to dry off and relax. "Let's rest on this hāpu'u fern," he said as he stretched out to feel the sun's warm rays.

"Is your valley named after this fern?" Kāhuli asked, admiring the delicately curled leaves.

"It sure is. Our valley used to be filled with them. Everywhere you looked you would find lush green hāpu'u ferns." Hau'oli looked at the devastated forest around him and sighed, "Now, there's only a few left in our entire valley."

"What happened to them?" Kāhuli wondered.

"They were destroyed by pigs!" Hau'oli said in disgust. "Those pigs are the worst! Since they came here, they've caused all kinds of damage to our forests. Our valley would never be in this terrible state if it weren't for those big, fat, ugly pigs!"

"Who are you calling ugly?!" bellowed a huge, ferocious pig hovering over them. "We'll see who's ugly when I get through with you!"

The pig dug his powerful tusks into the ground uprooting the fern with a single sweep. The force sent Kāhuli and Hauʻoli flying into the air. They landed near a withering ʻōhiʻa tree and quickly climbed to the top.

"We'll be safe up here," Hauʻoli said, trying to catch his breath.

Without a warning, they felt a . . . BOOM! The tree shook beneath them. Kāhuli looked down to see the pig charging the base of the tree.

BOOM! The pig continued to strike with full force, each crash loosening the tree's roots. Kāhuli knew the tree could only withstand a few more hits before toppling to the ground. This time there seemed to be no escape.

"What are we going to do now?" Kāhuli asked.

"I don't know," Hauʻoli replied. "But I'll think of something."

Above them, Hauʻoli saw a great pueo fly by.

"That's it!" he shouted, quickly spinning a web to make a lasso. "Hold on Kāhuli!"

With not a second to spare, he threw his lasso into the air. It barely caught onto the pueo's foot.

Below, the pig continued to charge. BOOM! One final blow sent the tree crashing to the ground just as Hauʻoli and Kāhuli were lifted into the sky.

"Look at the view!" Hauʻoli exclaimed as the pueo soared higher.

Kāhuli looked down and was reminded of his earlier fall. "I really would like to go home now," he said as he clung tightly to the silken web.

"Hey, maybe the pueo can help us," Hauʻoli said excitedly. "Excuse me, Miss Pueo!" he called out from below.

"Why hello," the pueo replied a bit surprised, "What are you two doing down there?"

"We're catching a ride, if you don't mind. And my friend here needs to get home to the Great ʻŌhiʻa Tree in ʻŌhiʻa Valley, would you mind taking us there?"

"Why I'd be happy to," the pueo said as she spread her powerful wings and headed for Kāhuli's homeland.

As they flew over the mountains and valleys, Kāhuli saw sights he had never seen before. All his life he had dreamed of seeing the world and now his dream had finally come true.

When they finally flew into ʻŌhiʻa Valley, Kāhuli was surprised to find that of all the sights he saw, the most spectacular was of his own home. Everything he had once taken for granted he now appreciated and cherished. He was especially happy to see the Great ʻŌhiʻa Tree standing proudly in the middle of the valley as it had for centuries. The pueo landed gently on the Great ʻŌhiʻa Tree and Kāhuli and Hauʻoli said their good-byes.

"Are you sure you can't stay?" Kāhuli asked hopefully.

"You know the rules," Hauʻoli replied.

"I know," Kāhuli continued as he climbed down onto the treetop, "everything must stay where they belong."

"That's right, Kāhuli. Never forget that."

The pueo once again spread her great wings and carried Hauʻoli off into the sky.

Kāhuli watched sadly as they disappeared beyond the mountains. He would miss his new friend, and yet he was happy to know that they would both be home, where they belonged. And as far as Kāhuli was concerned, there was nowhere else he would rather be than in the Great ʻŌhiʻa Tree.

Hawaiian Rainforest

Photo courtesy of DLNR, Division of Forestry and Wildlife, State of Hawai'i

Undisturbed for millions of years, the plants and animals that made their way to Hawai'i evolved into a variety of new species found nowhere else in the world. 90% of native Hawaiian plants and animals are found only in Hawai'i. The introduction of new species has played a major role in the decline of Hawaiian forests.

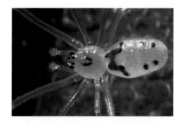

Kāhuli the O'ahu Tree Snail

Photo by William P. Mull

These rare native tree snails live in the forests on O'ahu. Each snail spends its entire lifetime on a single tree, carefully scouring and cleaning the leaves of harmful algae and molds. Often referred to as the "jewels of the Hawaiian forest", these ornamental snails average 3/4 inch in length and have smooth, glossy shells with a variety of patterns and colors. The rapid disappearance of these snails is attributed to over collection by humans, habitat destruction, and the introduction of predators such as rats and carnivorous snails. The entire genus of O'ahu tree snails has reached an endangered status. Of the 40 or more known species, over half are extinct and the remaining endangered.

Hau'oli the Happy-Face Spider

Photo by William P. Mull

Happy-Face spiders are native to Hawai'i and are not found anywhere else in the world. They are named for the variety of bright patterns on their abdomens that resemble smiling faces. These tiny spiders with bodies barely 1/4 inch long, are rarely seen. They live on the undersides of leaves, where their "happy face" patterns serve as a camouflage from predators. In the story, the happy-face spider is named Hau'oli, the Hawaiian word for "happy".

Pueo the Hawaiian Owl

Photo by Jack Jeffrey

The native pueo soars at very high altitudes and unlike most owls, the pueo is active during midday. There has been a decrease in the number of pueo on O'ahu due to loss of habitat, disease and misuse of pesticides.

'O'opu 'Alamo'o the Red-Tailed Goby

Photo by Mike Yamamoto, courtesy of Division of Aquatic Resources, State of Hawai'i

The 'o'opu 'alamo'o is one of five native gobies that live in Hawaiian streams. Their newly hatched larvae are swept downstream and out to sea. Several months later as juveniles, they return to the stream to live. Their suction cup fins enable them to crawl upstream and climb waterfalls. Human disturbances to stream beds have caused their population to decline.

Rosy the Cannibal Snail

Photo by Betsy Harrison Gagné

Rosy Glandina, commonly known as the cannibal snail, was brought in from Florida to eliminate the giant African snail. Unfortunately, these carnivorous snails attacked the native tree snails as well, causing some species to become extinct within a year. The cannibal snail continues to pose a serious threat to the remaining endangered tree snails in O'ahu's rainforests.

Rat

Photo by Jack Jeffrey

Three species of rats introduced to the islands inhabit Hawai'i today, the Norway Rat, the Black Rat, and the Polynesian Rat. The latter two have been found to cause severe damage to the forest's ecosystem by preying on native birds, eggs, snails and plants. Rat populations are extremely large in the rainforest.

Feral Pig

Photo by Jack Jeffrey

The feral pig is the rainforest's worst enemy. Domestic pigs were brought to Hawai'i by the Polynesians and Europeans, some of which escaped to the wild. Today thousands of pigs roam the forests, rooting up rare plants and large tree ferns, such as the native hāpu'u. These pigs leave muddied wallows that provide a breeding ground for mosquitos that transmit avian malaria to native birds. Pig wallows start erosion that washes mud and dirt into the streams, causing harm to the native fish and shrimp. The sediment travels downstream out to sea where it smothers the coral reefs.

A special thanks to:

Yukimasa and Jennifer Matsumoto

Seizo and Betty Furuya

Maile Sakamoto